Imagine what it will be like after Jesus comes . . .

SHELDON'S

Adventures in Heaven

Maxine Lois Wallace-Lang
Illustrated by Guy Porfirio

REVIEW AND HERALD® PUBLISHING ASSOCIATION
HAGERSTOWN, MD 21740

The author assumes full responsibility for the accuracy of all facts and quotations as cited in this book.

All Scripture references are from the *International Children's Bible, New Century Version,* copyright © 1983, 1986, 1988 by Word Publishing, Dallas, Texas 75039. Used by permission.

This book was
Edited by Jeannette R. Johnson
Designed by Mark O'Connor
Illustrations by Guy Porfirio
Typeset: 14/22 Hiroshige

PRINTED IN U.S.A.

07 06 05 04 03   5 4 3 2 1

R&H Cataloging Service
Wallace-Lang, Maxine L.
     Sheldon's adventures in heaven

          1. Heaven—Juvenile works.   I. Title.

                    236.24

ISBN 0-8280-1508-2

To order additional copies of *Sheldon's Adventures in Heaven,* by Maxine Lois Wallace-Lang, call **1-800-765-6955**.

Visit our website at www.rhpa.org for information on other Review and Herald® products.

A Special Gift

Just for you

_____

Lovingly presented

_____

"Let the little children come to me.
Don't stop them. The kingdom of God belongs to people
who are like these little children."
—Mark 10:14

Dedication

This book is dedicated to

God, our Father,

Jesus, our Friend,

and

the Holy Spirit, our Teacher,

in gratitude for

F. Sheldon Safrit

and

Caleb G. Safrit

Dear Mom and Dad

With longing hearts in these last days, we stand at the very edge of history, looking over into eternity.

How many times have you closed your eyes and allowed your quiet thoughts to take you to heaven's cool, green grass by the river of life?

You sit down under the tree of life and lean back against its trunk, looking up into the swaying branches and leaves . . . The fruit glistens with God's glory . . . Heaven's gentle breeze strokes your face . . .

We think of meeting God and talking face to face with Jesus . . . Walking with the Holy Spirit (what color is His hair?) . . . Singing with the angels—even playing with the animals.

With each dream our yearning grows stronger.

This little book is dedicated to helping you pass on to your children this warm, wonderful vision we now must carry in our hearts, not soon enough a reality. Young or old, we dream of heaven. I believe we honor God when we do so.

—Maxine Lois Wallace-Lang

Chapter One

Sheldon's Adventures in Heaven

Let the little children come to me. Don't stop them.
The kingdom of God belongs to people who are like
these little children. Mark 10:14.

Sheldon had always wanted to go to heaven. The great war on earth was finally over. Jesus came and took all the daddies, mommies, and little children who loved Him to heaven. He took anybody who wanted to love Him and live with Him.

"Sheldon, let's go and explore your new home!" Sheldon turned from the window to see Rapha coming through the front door. Rapha had been his guardian angel on earth, but now he was his "forever friend" in heaven.

"OK! I just have to tell Mommy." And off he went. Maybe today was the day he would find the pet bear he had always dreamed about. On earth he could have only a stuffed bear. But in heaven maybe he could have a *real* bear—big and white and cuddly and playful! And his name would be— Well, he would have to think about a name.

Mommy was working in her garden. She looked up and smiled when Sheldon and Rapha said they were going exploring. "That sounds like fun! Be home in time for dinner!"

And off they went while Mommy waved a handful of flowers after them.

They had a wonderful time! First they splashed in the lake, then sat on the shore and told stories. Next they climbed to a mountaintop before running all the way back down. They saw all kinds of animals, little and big—lions, tigers, lambs, giraffes, and birds. Some animals Sheldon had never seen or heard about. They had such fun with the animals.

But not one bear did they see.

Sheldon could fly now, if he wanted. And oh, he wanted to fly! He flew up, up, up to the treetops with Rapha.

But no bear was up there, either.

He met other boys and girls. They invited him to play with them,
but he couldn't. He was exploring.

And looking for his bear—his big white bear.

It was almost dinnertime when Sheldon had an idea: he would ask Jesus to show him where to find his bear. Jesus had *always* heard his prayers on earth when he needed help. Yes, he was sure Jesus would help.

They were nearing the Holy City, when Rapha saw Jesus sitting on the grass with a lot of children. The boys and girls were laughing and playing, rolling and tumbling, with all kinds of animals.

"Look! There's Jesus! What fun they're having!" Rapha shouted.

Sheldon ran over to them.

Jesus looked up and smiled a great big

The boys and girls were laughing and playing, rolling and tumbling, with all kinds of animals.

9

"His name is Keka."
Jesus smiled.
"And I love you,
Sheldon!"

smile. "Hello, Sheldon; come join us!"

Sheldon ran through the crowd of boys, girls, and animals and stopped right in front of Jesus.

Jesus laughed. "Did you have fun today with Rapha, exploring everything and everywhere? You're learning—but your discoveries have only begun!"

Sheldon was *trying* to listen to Jesus. But it was really hard to pay attention, because snuggled on Jesus' lap was a *bear,* a tiny baby bear! He was all white except for one little black ear. Sheldon had never seen anything like him on earth.

While He talked, Jesus scratched the little bear's ears and stroked his back. The little bear licked his paws and made funny noises and squirmed as close to Jesus as he could get.

Oh, Sheldon purely loved that little bear!

"Sheldon," Jesus said.

But Sheldon didn't hear Him. He was looking so hard he couldn't.

"Sheldon!" Jesus said again.

Then Sheldon heard Him. He looked up at Jesus and felt a big lump in his throat. He would love to ask Jesus if he could take that little bear home. But before Sheldon could even open his mouth to ask, Jesus was handing him the little bear.

"He'll grow up soon, and you'll be good friends—forever friends—like you and Rapha." Jesus' eyes twinkled, and He began talking again.

Sheldon tried to listen, but his heart was beating so fast. Mommy and Daddy would be so excited about his new friend! Sheldon thanked Jesus with a hug that was so big that his little bear, who was squeezed right in the middle of the hug, said, "Oooof!" Then Sheldon and Rapha turned to go home.

"Sheldon," called Jesus.

Sheldon turned to look at Jesus.

"His name is Keka." Jesus smiled. "And I love you, Sheldon!"

Chapter Two

Sheldon Plans a Trip

No one has ever seen this. No one has ever heard about it.
No one has ever imagined what God has prepared
for those who love him. 1 Corinthians 2:9.

Heaven had so many rocks! Sheldon really enjoyed his rock collection. He had green rocks, blue rocks, little black rocks, and big clear rocks. All of them shone and sparkled when he held them up to the light. Mommy said they were real gems that God had sprinkled all around heaven, just for them to enjoy. He had several shelves in his room, filled with his beautiful rocks.

Sheldon heard Daddy calling. "Come here, son; I have something to tell you!"

"I'm coming!" Sheldon answered, carefully replacing the rock he held in his hand.

"I have exciting news!" Daddy said, as Sheldon plopped himself down on a soft cushion. Keka crawled as close as he could and laid his snowy white head in Sheldon's lap. Gently Sheldon stroked Keka's black ear. Keka was really getting big!

Daddy's eyes sparkled. "Son, we are going to take a journey to another world, a world that God created that's much like our old earth was before sin ruined it." Daddy said they would be gone a long time, as there would be so much to learn and so many places to explore on this other world. Imagine! Another world far away!

While Mommy and Daddy were still talking about the wonderful trip, Sheldon ran back to his room. He needed to pack! He pulled out a small trunk and put two robes inside—one for Sabbath, and one for play. Then he put in his Sabbath sandals. And on top of everything he gently laid his beautiful crown . . . No! Wait! Maybe he'd wear his crown. He purely loved his crown! It had beautiful "rocks" on it that Jesus Himself had chosen.

Then Sheldon tucked in his favorite little books beside his robes and a couple small empty boxes (in case he found a new or different rock for his collection). He looked around the room to see if he had forgotten anything.

There was Keka, snoozing near the door.

"Uh, oh! What about Keka?"

Sheldon knew that he, Daddy, Mommy, and Rapha could easily fly to the other world. But what about Keka? Keka could run and climb trees. He had even learned to hang upside down from the tree limbs. Well, sort of. He knew how to play hide-and-seek. But Keka couldn't fly.

What to do? Keka was much too big now to snuggle in Sheldon's arms. But Sheldon couldn't even

No! Wait! Maybe he'd wear his crown. He purely loved his crown!

15

think about leaving him at home—Keka went *everywhere* Sheldon went. Keka was his very own pet bear. Keka was his forever friend.

Then Sheldon knew what to do. He would talk to Jesus! He ran from his room, down the hall, and through the great room, where Mommy and Daddy were still talking.

"Where are you going so fast, son?" Daddy called as Sheldon dashed past.

"To find Jesus! I've got to ask Him about Keka!"

Sheldon flew to the City and ran to God's house. He didn't have to wait long. Soon Jesus stepped onto the front porch, a smile lighting His face.

"Hello, Sheldon! I'm glad you came. Let's sit down here on the steps, and I will help you with Keka."

He knew! Jesus knew all about Keka before Sheldon had said a word! But Sheldon explained it all to Him anyway. How could Keka go with him on the long journey?

Jesus leaned back and stretched His legs out in front of Him. "Well, Sheldon, remember back on earth, just before I came to get you? You and your mommy and daddy were hiding from the bad people. Rapha was there to protect you. You couldn't see him then, but he was there beside you, covering you, watching over you, caring for you. He was your guardian angel. Then I came in the clouds with all the angels. Your mommy told you to look up! And just as you looked up to Me, Rapha reached out and wrapped his arm around your little shoulders and caught you up to meet Me in the air. You noticed Rapha then, didn't you?"

"Yes!" Sheldon said. "He was beautiful!"

Jesus laughed. "Yes, Rapha is beautiful and strong. And just as Rapha brought you to Me, well, that's how you can take Keka with you. Just wrap your little arm as far around Keka's furry shoulders as you can, and off you'll go! You won't get tired, and he won't fall."

Then Jesus invited Sheldon to go for a walk. He wanted to show Sheldon *His* rock collection. So off they went, toward the great gates of the City.

Jesus had answers to every question. And it was so much fun being with Him! Sheldon purely loved Jesus!

It had beautiful "rocks" on it that Jesus had chosen Himself.

Sheldon Visits Another World

It is by faith we understand that the whole world was made by God's command. Hebrews 11:3.

Sheldon's little trunk was packed and waiting by the door. Mommy and Daddy were almost ready to go too, so Sheldon went to find his friends to say goodbye. He was so excited about his trip to Sarta! He had many friends in heaven, but closest to his heart was Rukoh. Rukoh and his little brother Ron spent a lot of time up in Sheldon's tree house or playing treetop tag with Keka and Jordon, Rukoh and Ron's pet tiger. Every day the three boys would fly to school together. Rukoh and Ron were happy for Sheldon. They were all excited

Keka loved the water, so it was hard for him to sit still in the boat. Finally he jumped overboard.

about his trip to Sarta!

Jesus said Sheldon would have fun and learn a lot. He told him to be sure to take several boxes, because Sarta had very beautiful rocks he would want for his collection.

Rapha went with Sheldon, Mommy, Daddy, and Keka to the travel station. There Angel Mara would transport them to Sarta.

When they arrived, Sheldon was beside himself with excitement! He saw that Sarta had seven moons, large and bright! The grass looked so green and soft that he just had to take his sandals off. The grass was cool under his toes. He saw and heard little birds that he had never seen or heard before. What a wonderful place God had made!

Sarta even had a tree of life, just like the one in heaven! It was at the tree of life that Sheldon met a new friend. Caleb was very friendly and kind. He offered to take Sheldon exploring, and he asked Sheldon to stay at his home. He said Sheldon's mommy and daddy were welcome too.

They had so much fun! Caleb had two fluffy little black and brown dogs—Maru and Beauty. They knew how to play a lot of games, but their favorite game was tug-a-rope.

The best time of all came when Caleb, Sheldon, Keka, Maru, and Beauty went to the Lake of Lights. Everyone went to the lake for a picnic. The lake water was crystal clear. You could see all the way to the bottom. But yet the water looked blue, then green, and sometimes violet. Sheldon saw all colors. The sun shone on the lake, making little sparkling lights everywhere.

Caleb ran to a boat that was tied to a tree. "Let's go to the middle of the lake. I'll show you why the water changes color and sparkles!"

Everyone climbed into the boat. Daddy untied the cord and climbed in too, and off they paddled. Keka loved water, so it was hard for him to sit still in the boat. Finally he jumped overboard. Then into the lake went Maru and Beauty, right behind Keka! They all splashed and played

and swam around the boat.

Caleb turned to Sheldon. "Come on! Let's dive down to the bottom. You'll see beautiful rocks."

Over the side of the boat they went, and down, down, down. Caleb gathered a handful of rocks. Sheldon did too. Then with a mighty push with their feet, they slipped through the water, up to the boat.

Sheldon studied his rocks closely. They were all alike, only different in size and shape. All were clear as glass. Sheldon could see through them, but if he turned his head a little or tipped the rock, they flashed all different colors of the rainbow! Caleb was watching Sheldon study his rocks. "Do you see now what makes the lake water different colors? And the sun shining on them through the water movement makes them sparkle."

"Oh, yes!" Sheldon said. "I'll need more!"

Back down they went. He gathered rocks for his friends back home. And he chose a large one to take to God, and one for Jesus, and one for the Holy Spirit.

When they were through collecting rocks and playing in the lake with Keka and the dogs, they paddled to shore to have their picnic of wonderful sweet, juicy fruits that Sheldon had never tasted before—and manna cakes. His favorite! Keka, Maru, and Beauty curled up together on the edge of the picnic blanket in the sunshine and munched manna cakes too.

Sheldon was so happy! He couldn't wait to show Jesus his new rocks.

Sheldon loved the planet Sarta. Sheldon purely loved God the Creator.

Sheldon could see through them, but if he turned his head a little or tipped the rock, they flashed all different colors of the rainbow!

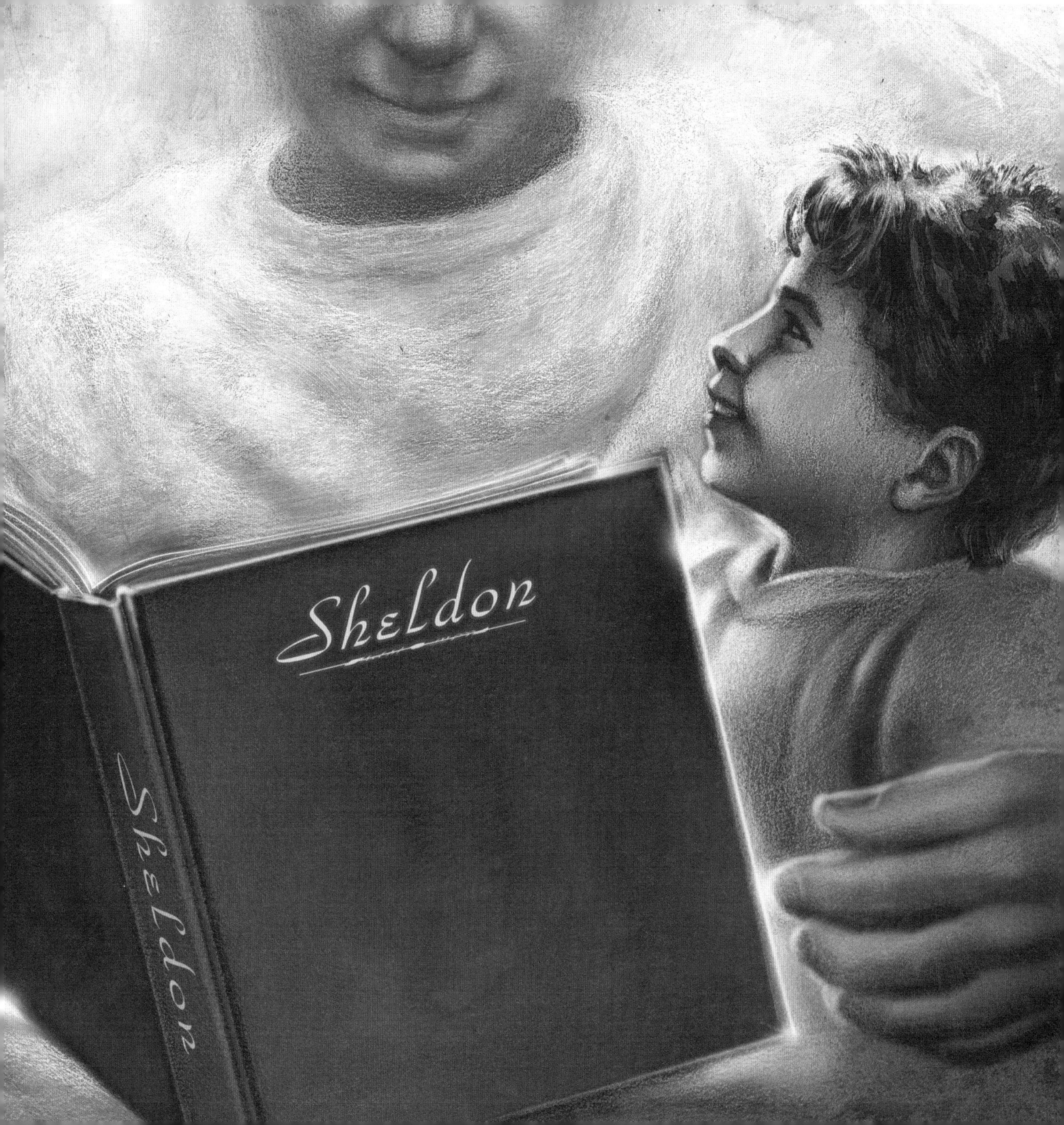
Sheldon
Sheldon

Sheldon Meets God

The names of those who honored the Lord and respected him were written in a book. The Lord will remember them. The Lord of heaven's armies says, "They belong to me." Malachi 3:16, 17.

Sheldon thought heaven was so much fun! He had been hanging upside down in the tall tree in the front yard all morning. Keka was doing pretty well at hanging upside down too, but even so, Rapha stood under the tree limb to catch him when he fell. Keka knew how to climb trees, but hanging upside down was something the little bear would have to practice more.

"Sheldon!" Mommy was calling. She came to the window just in time to see Keka drop once more into Rapha's strong arms. "Come in now! We are getting ready to go to the City. This is a very special day: today is your time to meet with God! He is going to show you your book."

Jesus handed Sheldon a big book. The front of the book had Sheldon's name written on it in big golden letters right above his birth date.

Sheldon dashed inside the house. He ran to his room and changed into his Sabbath robe. Carefully he tied the blue belt. Then he hung up his play clothes. He got distracted only once when a little snow-white bird landed on his window ledge and sang him a happy song. He combed his hair, then ran to the shelf and reached for his crown.

He loved his beautiful crown! Jesus had given

it to him on his very first day in heaven. His finger traced its golden smoothness and bumped over the brightly colored stones (Mommy called them gems) and little white stars. And there—right in the middle—was his name, his very own *new* name, right next to Jesus' name. Sheldon took his crown to Mommy, and she smoothed his hair a little more (because mommies have to do that). Then she placed that golden crown on his head and gave him a big hug and kiss (because mommies have to do that, too!).

They stepped out onto the porch, where Daddy was talking to Rapha. Sheldon slipped his hand into Daddy's hand, and off they went to meet God.

God's house was beautiful—big and shining and full of light. Great golden doors in front opened wide. People and angels were everywhere. Angel Zerah met them and took them to the great white throne where God meets with all those who love Him.

Sheldon looked up. There was God. And Jesus was right next to Him. Sheldon stared at the beautiful rainbow that made a big circle around the throne. Mommy, Daddy, and Sheldon bowed before God.

"Welcome to our home!" God's voice was big and warm and gentle.

God smiled at Sheldon. He held out His hand. "Come, Sheldon; come and sit between Us. I have something to show you."

Then God wrapped His arm around Sheldon and drew him a little closer. Jesus handed Sheldon a big book. The front of the book had Sheldon's name written on it in big golden letters, right above his birth date.

Jesus opened the book. God turned the first page and began to read.

He read how Mommy and Daddy had taken care of Sheldon—when he slept and played, when he ate and started to walk and talk. God read about Sheldon growing day by day—every word he said, everything he did, everything he thought, and every prayer he prayed. God read about every commandment he kept, each time he helped Mommy with the dishes or cleaned his room without fussing, each time he obeyed Daddy, and every dime, nickel, or penny he put in the offering at church.

Sheldon saw everything all written down. But every once in a while he saw a blank spot on the page. So Sheldon asked God what those blank spots were.

God gave him a little squeeze and smiled. "Those times you were naughty or disobedient, or lied or were mean to someone, the angel wrote that down too. But when you said you were sorry and asked Jesus to forgive you, We *did* forgive you and took it out of your book."

Sheldon smiled. He was glad he had asked Jesus to forgive him!

God went on reading. Before long He turned the last page and closed the book.

Sheldon looked up at Jesus. He smiled.

Then Sheldon looked up into God's face. Gently God put His big hands on each side of Sheldon's face and smiled down at Sheldon with His loving, kind eyes.

"Well done, Sheldon," God said. "Well done, my little son."

"Well done, Sheldon," God said. "Well done, my little son."

Sheldon

Chapter Five

Sheldon Goes to School

For you who honor me, goodness will shine on you like the sun.
There will be healing in its rays. You will jump around,
like calves freed from their stalls. Malachi 4:2.

Sheldon, Rapha, and Keka had wonderful adventures in heaven! They hiked into the woods, collected rocks, and played games Rapha would teach them. And no matter what Sheldon did or where he went, Keka was with him.

But storytime with God was probably Sheldon's most favorite thing to do. Once a week all the children in heaven met with God, and He'd tell wonderful stories! God's laughter would echo all through heaven! Sometimes Keka would snuggle close, and God would scratch his little black ear. Then he'd lie down at God's feet.

Sometimes Sheldon visited Grandma and Grandpa's house. They always brought a picnic lunch to eat by the waterfall on the way. Sheldon and Keka splashed and splattered water everywhere as they ran up and down in the little stream. Then Keka would sit in the very middle of the waterfall, making funny little happy noises, while the water tumbled over his head.

When they were through playing, Keka would lie down on Mommy's picnic blanket next to Sheldon and eat plump, juicy grapes and manna cakes. Keka loved Sheldon. And Sheldon purely loved Keka and manna cakes!

One day Mommy came into Sheldon's room with an important announcement. "Guess what! Angel Zerah has just come with the message that school will start soon in the City."

"School!" Sheldon exclaimed. "School in *heaven?*"

Sure," Mommy said. "You'll learn lots of things. Think about what fun field trips will be! And you'll learn to play your harp and sing like the angels. Jesus will teach too, and God will visit the school often. You'll learn about other worlds and the love of God. It's so exciting! Why,

Mommy and Daddy will go to school too! Everybody who came to heaven will go to school."

Sheldon thought for a minute. "All right. I think school will be fun— especially with Mommy and Daddy as students too!"

Finally the first day of school came. SnowDrop, the little snow-white bird that lived near his window ledge, sang a sweet song for him while he got ready. After he combed his hair, he decided to wear his crown on this first day of school.

Keka waited under the window ledge, watching SnowDrop. She jumped down and landed on his head, between his little ears, to finish singing her song. Sheldon laughed. "You two must stay here and keep each other company today, because I get to go to school!"

She jumped down and landed on his head, between his little ears, to finish singing her song.

Daddy stuck his head around the corner. "Ready, Sheldon?" He reached out for Sheldon's hand. "Let's go!"

Keka and SnowDrop watched them disappear. They watched for a long time, but Sheldon didn't come back. They watched for a *very* long time, but Sheldon still didn't come back. Keka decided to go find Sheldon. So with SnowDrop still standing on his head, he put his nose to the ground and ambled off in search of his friend.

When Keka and SnowDrop got near the school, Keka thought he heard Sheldon's voice and followed the sound of singing. He was right! Sheldon had joined choir practice because he wanted to sing praises to God.

Slowly Keka walked through the big open doors of the schoolhouse. SnowDrop was very quiet. Keka was quiet too, following the sound of Sheldon's voice. He peeked his head around the door of the choir room and, sure enough! There was Sheldon! Keka was so happy to see his friend that he threw his head up into the air and started "singing" too! Then SnowDrop started singing. They sang and sang!

Angel Zerah, who was directing the choir, stopped short and turned around to look. The children stopped singing. Then Keka and SnowDrop stopped singing. It became very quiet as everyone looked at Keka and SnowDrop. Sheldon looked at Angel Zerah, and Angel Zerah turned and looked at Sheldon.

Angel Zerah smiled. "It looks as though we have two new students!"

Sheldon's heart leaped for joy. He was so happy Angel Zerah didn't mind that Keka and SnowDrop had tried to join the choir. But after that, if Keka and SnowDrop wanted to go to school, they had to wait quietly on the lawn by the front door or under Sheldon's desk until play time.

Sheldon loved Angel Zerah. Sheldon loved school. Sheldon purely loved heaven.

Sheldon looked at Angel Zerah, and Angel Zerah turned and looked at Sheldon.

35

The Tree of Life

The angel showed me the river of the water of life. The river was shining like crystal. It flows from the throne of God and of the Lamb down the middle of the street of the city. The tree of life was on each side of the river. It produces fruit 12 times a year, once each month. Revelation 22:1, 2.

There probably was not a more wonderful place to go and visit in all of heaven than the tree of life. It grew a different fruit each month. Its fruit was sweet and juicy, and the tree grew on both sides of the river of life. Sheldon loved going there with Mommy, and he loved climbing the tree. You never knew who you would see there. Maybe Daniel with his pet lion. Maybe Esther or Jonah or Samson or Abraham—or even God Himself.

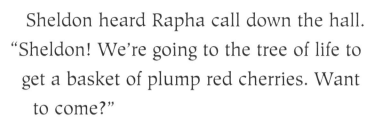

Sheldon heard Rapha call down the hall. "Sheldon! We're going to the tree of life to get a basket of plump red cherries. Want to come?"

Sheldon was sitting on his bed, looking at a book. "Yeah! I'll be right there!"

Suddenly Rukoh flew in through Sheldon's window and bounced on the bed. He bounced so hard that it bounced Sheldon right off and onto the floor! Rukoh laughed so hard that he rolled onto the floor next to Sheldon. Sheldon was laughing now too. Rukoh always (well, almost always) visited Sheldon this way.

Keka shuffled over to the window and looked out just as Sheldon's friend, Ron, flew through and pounced on him. Boy and bear tumbled over and over across the room. Mommy came to see what all the thumps and giggles were about.

"I thought so!" she laughed. "Rukoh, it's nice to see you and Ron again. Do you two think you'll ever use the front door?" Rukoh laughed. "Probably not as long as I can still fit through Sheldon's window! It's so much fun!"

*J*ust then, in came Stephen through the window. As he bounced off the bed, in flew Jason, then Amber, Tom, and Lettie.

Mommy threw her hands up. "Sheldon, it looks like you need a bigger room!"

Kids and giggles were everywhere.

"All right," Mommy said. "We will *all* go to the tree of life! OK?"

"YEAH!" they all shouted together.

"Want to fly or walk?" Mommy asked as she reached for Sheldon's hand.

"Fly!" Sheldon replied.

And off they all flew, while Keka and Jordon ran as fast as they could on the ground below.

When they all arrived at the tree of life, they saw Jesus sitting on the bank of the river, under the tree. He was eating the plump red cherries. He would eat one, then hold out His hand, and another cherry would drop into His hand. He'd eat it, and

"Want to fly or walk?" Mommy asked as she reached for Sheldon's hand. "Fly!" Sheldon replied.

hold out His hand again.

Puzzled, Sheldon decided to climb up and see where the cherries were coming from. Up in the highest branches, fluttering around, was SnowDrop. Sheldon watched her pluck a cherry with her beak and drop it—right into Jesus' hand! Sheldon whistled at SnowDrop and looked down.

Jesus smiled up at him and waved.

Sheldon waved back and dropped a cherry into His hand. Then he climbed down from the tree and began helping Mommy by picking cherries and dropping them into her basket. Soon all the children were picking cherries to take home.

Then Sheldon heard Jesus laugh. Then He laughed again. Sheldon went to see what was so funny. Now SnowDrop was not only dropping cherries, she was racing them down to Jesus' hand. And sometimes she would almost get to His hand before the cherry did!

When SnowDrop flew back up for another cherry, Sheldon called to her. "Wait! Wait, SnowDrop. I have a fun idea! We'll both drop cherries and see who gets to Jesus first—us or the cherries!"

Sheldon flew to the very top of the tree. SnowDrop picked her cherry; Sheldon picked his cherry. He counted "1-2-3" and the cherries fell. Sheldon and SnowDrop swooped out of the treetop, racing those cherries down! Jesus looked up and saw them coming through the branches and leaves. He stood up, opened His arms, and Sheldon and SnowDrop and two plump cherries fell right into them. Jesus hugged them tight, whirled around, and fell backward—right into the river!

Jesus came out of the water, laughing and wiping His face. Sheldon came up laughing and sputtering! SnowDrop chirped and fluttered her wings. And all of Sheldon's friends, watching from the side of the river, laughed.

When all three were finished splashing and chasing each other, they sat down on the bank to dry off. Then Jesus and Sheldon, Rukoh and Ron, and all the other children ate plump, juicy cherries from the basket Rapha brought to them.

Sheldon loved his friends. Sheldon loved Jesus and the tree of life.

And Jesus purely loved plump red cherries!

Jesus looked up and saw them coming through the branches and leaves.

Chapter Seven

The New Home

From long ago no one has ever heard of a God like you.
No one has ever seen a God besides you.
You help the people who trust you. Isaiah 64:4.

Heaven was abuzz! Angels and people were busily planning and talking about a new home and the journey there.

"Rapha, what's happening?" Sheldon asked as Rapha came into the house one day.

"Well, Sheldon, the time has come for God to take us down to the old earth and finish the work there. The books have all been reviewed, and God must finish His work of judgment so He can re-create a new home for all of us. He will put away Satan and all sin forever."

The sky turned crystal blue and lofty mountains rose out of the ashes. Trees, shrubs, flowers, streams, lakes, and waterfalls appeared everywhere.

"Oh! Will I go down to the old earth too? Will I watch what God does? Will I see Satan and his bad angels and all the bad people?" Sheldon asked.

"Yes, yes, and yes!" said Rapha, smiling. "We will all go and watch."

Sheldon threw his arms around Rapha's waist. "I won't be afraid. I have you and Mommy and Daddy and Jesus. I know God loves us and won't let the bad people hurt us again."

"That's right." Rapha hugged Sheldon for a long time.

Then Keka licked Sheldon in the face and made him giggle.

The big day finally came. Mommy and Daddy were ready. Rapha took Sheldon's hand. "Let's go to the City," he said. Keka followed close beside Sheldon with SnowDrop nestled in her favorite spot on Keka's head.

In the City they gathered around God's great throne. God told them what was going to happen. He said that Jesus was already on His way down to earth to make a place for the City.

Then God raised His great arms high, and everyone started singing and rising up, high above the City, for the journey down to earth. Sheldon watched as the great gates of the City were closed tight. Angels were all around the people. The great City began to move down, down, down, closer to earth, right behind Jesus. All the people and angels followed.

Everything happened just as God had said. God made all the bad people alive again so He could show them their books of remembrance, where all their sins were written down. God wanted them to see Jesus get His crown and see all the happy people inside the City. They would know what they were going to miss because they hadn't wanted to love Jesus.

Then fire came down from God and started burning everything—the ugly old earth, all the bad people, the bad angels, and Satan. The fire got bigger and hotter, but Sheldon and Rapha, Mommy and Daddy, and all of God's people were safe inside the City. God told them how much He loved them and promised to keep them safe.

And He did.

When the fire was all gone, nothing but cold ashes was left. God asked for the gates of the City to be opened. God, Jesus, and the Holy Spirit went out and talked for a while.

Rapha looked at Sheldon. "Watch! Now God will make our new home."

Sheldon watched. God and Jesus spoke to each other; then Jesus turned and spoke to the Holy Spirit. When the Holy Spirit raised His arm, it all began to happen.

The sky turned crystal blue, and lofty mountains rose out of the ashes. Beautiful green grass spread under their feet. Trees, shrubs, flowers, streams, lakes, and waterfalls appeared everywhere!

Sheldon could hardly stand it! Rapha and all the angels started singing praises. The people started singing. Even Keka and SnowDrop were so happy about their new home that they tried to sing too.

Sheldon loved Jesus. Sheldon loved the Holy Spirit. And Sheldon purely loved God.

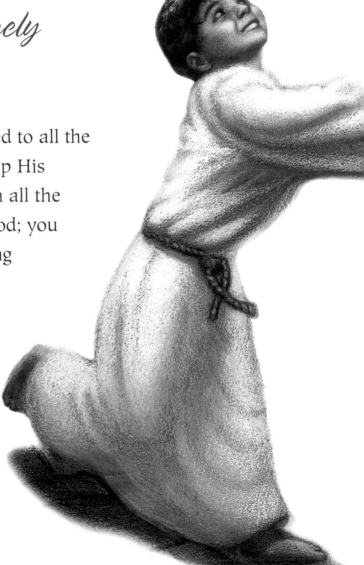

Then all became quiet. God turned to all the people. He was smiling, and raised up His arms. His great voice echoed through all the earth: "I am your Father and your God; you are My children, and I will live among you. I love you. Welcome home!"

Sheldon's heart leaped for joy! He wanted to run and hug God around His waist.

Sheldon loved Jesus. Sheldon loved the Holy Spirit. And Sheldon purely loved God.

47

I am
your Father
and your God;
you are my child,
and I will live
among you.
I love you.
Welcome home!